# Angel
# Prayers

# Angel Prayers

## Prayers for All Children

by Susan Heyboer O'Keefe

Illustrated by Sofia Suzán

Boyds Mills Press

Text copyright © 1999 by Susan Heyboer O'Keefe
Illustrations copyright © 1999 by Sofia Suzán
All rights reserved

Published by Caroline House
Boyds Mills Press, Inc.
A Highlights Company
815 Church Street
Honesdale, Pennsylvania 18431
Printed in China

Publisher Cataloging in Publication Data
O'Keefe, Susan Heyboer.
  Angel prayers : prayers for all children / by Susan Heyboer O'Keefe ;
illustrated by Sofia Suzán.—1st ed.
   [32]p. : col. Ill.;   cm.
Summary: A collection of original prayers for young pre-school and early
grade children.
ISBN 1-56397-683-8
1. Prayers—Juvenile literature. [1. Prayers.] I. Suzán, Sofia, ill.
II. Title.
291.4 —dc21   1999   AC   CIP

Library of Congress Catalog Card Number  98-88220

First edition, 1999
The text of this book is set in 24-point Optima.
The illustrations are done in acrylic.

10 9 8 7 6 5 4 3 2 1

To the three O'Keefe angels: Megan, Erin, and Emily

—S. H. O'K.

To my mother, Amalia,
who has been and always will be my guardian angel

—S. S.

There's a little bit of angel
deep inside of you,
a little pair of wings
trying to poke through,
a little bit of angel
that wants so much to be
just like the real angels
who care for you and me.

Good morning, angel,
bless my day
as I work
and as I play.
Everything
I see and do
and hear and say—
bless that, too.

Bless the family I live with,
the family I play with,
the family I learn with,
the family I pray with.

Angel, please stay close to me.

Watch the things I do and see.

Guide my feet and light my way.

Tell me when it's time to pray.

Always help me do what's right.

And keep me safe both day and night.

When I'm lonely,
when I'm sad,
when I'm hurt,
or when I'm mad,
help me see
I'm not alone.
I have an angel
all my own.

Cherubim

Seraphim

Thrones

Dominions

Virtues

Powers

Principalities
Archangels
Angels

Help me be an angel
to someone else today,
someone kind and loving
whose feet have lost their way.
Help me help this someone
to see within my face
an angel all their own
that waits to take my place.

Thank you, God,
for everything:
for puddles
and pets
and angel wings,
for candy
and kites
and bugs
that don't bite.
Thank you, God,
for everything.

Make me as happy
as an angel at play.
Make me as thankful
as an angel at prayer.
Make me as loving
as an angel at work.
Make me as brave
as an angel mid-air.

I'm sorry, God, for what I did.

I'm sorry for what I said.

I'm sorry for every tear
I made my angel shed.

Help me do better tomorrow.

Help me do all I should do.

Help me remember that You love me
even more than I love You.

Thank you, angel, for being here,
for staying at my side,
for making me brave,
for keeping me true,
for never letting me hide.
Thank you, angel, for being here,
my wonderful secret friend.
Thank you for helping me every day
from morning till the night's end.

Let me remember
each stranger I see
just might be an angel
who's come to help me.

Let me rest in your hand, God.
Let me sleep in Your love.
Now send me an angel
with the wings of a dove.
Have it stand by my side
throughout the long night.
Let it watch over my dreams
till morning brings light.

## About Angels

Angels are messengers from God. They guide and protect us. They bring us comfort, hope, and peace. Almost every religion and culture in the world believes in them.

Some people think we each have a guardian angel who stays with us at every moment. Others think angels come only when we need them. Whichever is true, angels visit us in many ways. They may come to us in a dream. They may be a whisper, even though no one is there. They may appear in a vision, which is like a dream when we're awake. Or they may disguise themselves as an ordinary man, woman, or child to help us.

In the end, angels are a mystery. And the only thing we may ever really discover about them is that they are messengers of God's love.

—Susan